MARVIN REDPOST 3

Is He a Girl?

by Louis Sachar

illustrated by Barbara Sullivan

A STEPPING STONE BOOK™

Random House New York

To Jonathan and Erin

Text copyright © 1993 by Louis Sachar.
Illustrations copyright © 1993 by Barbara Sullivan.
Cover illustration copyright © 1993 by Neal Hughes.
Published in the United States by Random House Children's Books, a division of
Random House, Inc., New York, and simultaneously in Canada by Random House
of Canada Limited, Toronto.

www.randomhouse.com/kids

Library of Congress Cataloging-in-Publication Data
Sachar, Louis. Marvin Redpost : is he a girl? / by Louis Sachar ;
illustrated by Barbara Sullivan.
  p. cm. A stepping stone book.
SUMMARY: After Casey Happleton tells him that if he kisses his elbow he will turn
into a girl, nine-year-old Marvin experiments and finds himself very confused about
his identity.
ISBN 0-679-81948-7 (trade) — ISBN 0-679-91948-1 (lib. bdg.)
[1. Sex role—Fiction. 2. Identity—Fiction. 3. Schools—Fiction.]
I. Sullivan, Barbara, ill. II. Title.
PZ7.S1185Map 1993 [Fic]—dc20 92-40784

Printed in the United States of America
29 28 27 26 25 24 23 22 21

Random House, Inc. New York, Toronto, London, Sydney, Auckland

Contents

1

A Weird Girl

Casey Happleton said, "If you kiss yourself on the elbow, you'll turn into a girl."

Marvin Redpost looked at her.

They sat next to each other in Mrs. North's class.

Casey had a ponytail that stuck out of the side of her head, instead of the back.

"It's true," said Casey. "If a boy kisses his elbow, he'll turn into a girl. And if a girl kisses her elbow, she'll turn into a boy."

"Can you change back?" asked Marvin.

"Sure," said Casey. "You just have to kiss your elbow again."

Marvin thought about it. But he wasn't about to try.

At least not in front of Casey.

"Does it matter which elbow you kiss?" he asked.

"Either one," said Casey. "But it has to be on the outside, where it's hard. Not the soft part on the inside."

"Have you ever kissed your elbow?" Marvin asked her.

"No!" she exclaimed. "What do you think I am—some kind of weirdo?"

Marvin shrugged. He did think Casey Happleton was weird.

"Who's jabbering?" asked Mrs. North. "Marvin and Casey?"

Marvin turned red. Everyone was looking at him and Casey. He hoped no one thought he liked her.

He folded his arms on his desk, and lay his head on top of them.

He looked at his elbow.

First of all, he didn't believe he'd really turn into a girl.

Second of all, he didn't know if his mouth could even reach his elbow.

He slowly moved his mouth toward his elbow. He wasn't going to kiss it. He just wanted to see if his mouth would reach.

It didn't.

He tried a different way. He sat up straight. Then he reached behind himself, as if to scratch his back.

He stretched out his lips.

"Oh my gosh!" said Casey. She bit her finger.

"What?" Marvin demanded.

"I saw you!" said Casey. "You were trying to kiss your elbow."

"I was not," said Marvin. "I was scratching my back."

"You want to be a girl!" said Casey.

"I had an itch," said Marvin.

"You're so weird," said Casey.

"You're the one who's weird," said Marvin. "You think everyone who scratches his back is really trying to kiss his elbow."

"Not everyone," said Casey. "Just you."

"Marvin! Casey!" said Mrs. North. "Do I have to separate you two?"

"Oooh, Marvin and Casey!" said Judy.

The other kids laughed.

Marvin buried his head under his arms.

She's the one who's weird, he thought. *I would never try to turn into a girl right in the middle of class! I wouldn't change into a girl anyway. But if I did, I wouldn't do it in school!*

"Casey," Melanie said, loud enough for Marvin to hear. "I think Marvin likes you."

Casey looked at Marvin. "Oh my gosh," she said. She bit her finger.

That was another reason Marvin thought Casey was weird. She always said "Oh my gosh" and bit her finger. And her sideways ponytail was weird, too!

The bell rang. He went outside to recess.

"What were you and Casey talking about?" asked Stuart. Stuart Albright was Marvin's best friend.

"Nothing," said Marvin. "She's so weird."

"You don't *like* her, do you?" asked Nick. Nick Tuffle was also Marvin's best friend.

"No way!" said Marvin. "You want to hear what she said?"

"What?" asked his two best friends.

"It's so weird," said Marvin. "She said—" He stopped. "She said she talks to dogs and cats!"

Nick and Stuart laughed.

"How weird!" said Stuart.

"She's so weird," said Nick.

They got in line to play wall-ball.

Marvin didn't know why he had lied to his two best friends.

2
Bugged

Marvin Redpost lived in a two-story gray house. There was a fence around the house. The fence was all white except for one red post next to the gate.

Marvin tapped the red post as he walked through the gate.

He stopped outside the front door. He tried kissing his elbow again.

"What are you doing, Mar?" asked Jacob, coming home behind him.

Jacob was Marvin's older brother.

Marvin froze. "Uh . . ." he said. He looked at his bent arm. "I'm practicing karate."

"Cool," said Jacob.

They walked inside together. Marvin admired his older brother. Jacob was cool.

There was no way Jacob would ever try to kiss *his* elbow.

Marvin also had a little sister named Linzy. Linzy was four.

"I got a sticker," Linzy said.

"Good," said Marvin. He set down his books on the kitchen counter.

"You can't have it," said Linzy.

"I don't want it," Marvin assured her.

"I'm telling!" Linzy snapped.

"What?" asked Marvin.

"Mommy!" Linzy shouted.

Their mother came into the kitchen.

"Marvin said he didn't like my sticker!" said Linzy. "He said it was a *stupid sticker*!"

"I never said that," said Marvin.

"Linzy earned that sticker in gymnastics," Mrs. Redpost said proudly.

"That's good, Linzy," said Marvin.

"Watch," said Linzy.

Marvin watched his sister do a somersault in the hall.

"That's great, Linzy!" he told her.

He meant it, too.

Marvin couldn't do a somersault. He just thought girls were better at somersaults than boys.

Just before going to bed, Marvin tried to kiss his elbow *one more time.*

He'd been trying all evening. Between homework problems. Before and after he brushed his teeth. While feeding General Jackson.

General Jackson was his pet lizard. The General lived in a glass cage next to Marvin's desk.

"This is stupid," Marvin told General

9

Jackson. "Even if I could kiss my elbow, nothing would happen."

General Jackson stuck out his tongue.

Marvin was wearing Ninja Turtle pajamas.

He liked being a boy. He was glad he was a boy! Girls were stupid and weird. One thing for sure. He did not want to turn into a girl!

At least not forever. Maybe it would be okay for a few minutes. Just to see what it was like.

But you can't turn into a girl just by kissing your elbow, he thought. That was stupid. Casey Happleton was stupid. Why would anyone want to turn into a girl if girls were always saying stupid things like that?

He tried kissing his elbow again.

It just bugged him that he couldn't do it.

It was twelve o'clock. Midnight.

Marvin lay asleep, all twisted and tangled in his sheets. He was hugging his pillow.

A full moon shone through the window.

He rolled over. Then he flopped back the other way.

As he rolled and flopped around in his bed, he got more and more tangled in his sheets.

Then, still hugging his pillow, he rolled right off the edge of the bed.

But he never hit the floor. He was so tangled that the sheets held him up.

"Huh-wha'?" he said.

He found himself hanging upside down. All wrapped up like a mummy.

He tried to get back onto the bed. He pulled a sheet.

Suddenly his elbow was jerked almost to his mouth. Then it bounced back.

He tugged the sheet again.

Again his elbow jerked to his mouth.

He pulled, then kept on pulling, harder
and harder.

His elbow moved closer and closer.

It felt like his arm was breaking.

He stretched out his lips.

It felt like his shoulder was about to pop out.

He gave it one hard yank!

The sheet pulled out from under the mattress. He fell to the floor.

But as his head hit the carpet, he kissed himself on the elbow.

3

Marvin Wears a Dress

Marvin got up. He checked himself over. He was still a boy.

Of course he was still a boy!

He couldn't wait to tell Casey. That would prove once and for all she was weird.

He climbed back into bed.

No, he couldn't tell Casey, he realized. Then she'd think he was weird for kissing his elbow.

But he had done it. That was the main thing.

There's nothing Marvin Redpost can't do! he thought.

He went right to sleep.

He dreamed he was playing baseball.

The bases were loaded. Two outs. Last inning. His team was losing by three runs.

A home run would win the game.

"Good. Marvin's up," said Nick. "Marvin will hit a home run."

"There's nothing Marvin Redpost can't do," said Stuart.

"It's his elbows," said Nick. "He has the strongest elbows on the team."

Marvin stepped up to the plate.

The crowd was cheering, "Mar-*vin*! Mar-*vin*! Mar-*vin*!"

Clarence was the pitcher. Clarence was the toughest kid in Marvin's class. Maybe in the whole school.

Marvin tapped the plate with his bat. He raised it above his shoulder.

Clarence spat on the dirt. He glared at Marvin.

Marvin waved the bat back and forth. He was afraid of Clarence but tried not to show it.

Suddenly Clarence laughed.

Then everyone else laughed too.

The umpire spoke to Marvin. "I'm sorry, young man," he said. "But you can't play. You're out of uniform."

"Huh?" said Marvin.

He looked down at his clothes. He was wearing a dress.

4

Don't Go to Sleep!

Marvin woke up screaming.

His mother came running up the stairs. "Linzy?" she called. "Linzy, are you all right?"

"It wasn't Linzy," Marvin called to her. "It was me, Marvin."

"Marvin?" asked his mother. She opened the door to his room.

"I had a nightmare," Marvin explained.

"Do you want to talk about it?"

"No!" Marvin said right away. He couldn't tell his mother that he wore a dress!

"I'm okay," he said.

His mother kissed his forehead. "Good

night," she said, and started out the door.

"Why'd you think I was Linzy?" Marvin asked.

"I don't know," said his mother. "You sounded like Linzy. Go back to sleep."

But he didn't go back to sleep.

He was afraid of turning into a girl.

"It's already started," he said aloud. "I already sound like a girl."

That's what his mother had said.

"I sound like Linzy."

He listened to the sound of his voice as he spoke. To see if it was true.

Maybe. It was hard to tell.

He spoke some more. "Mary had a little lamb. Her fleece was white as snow."

His voice did sound a little bit funny.

"Wait! Why am I talking about Mary and her dumb lamb?"

That's a girl poem!

But his voice did sound different. He was sure of it!

In school his class had been learning about butterflies and moths. A caterpillar goes to sleep. And when it wakes up, it's a butterfly.

He remembered Mrs. North had said, "No one knows exactly how a caterpillar turns into a butterfly."

Now Marvin had an answer.

Maybe it kisses its elbow.

He got out of bed.

He felt safe, as long as he was awake. He just couldn't go to sleep. Not until he kissed his elbow again.

Two hours later he was still trying to kiss his elbow.

He held his elbow in front of his face and jumped up and down. He thought that maybe if he could jump high enough and fast enough, his mouth would bump into it.

He stopped jumping. He looked at his bed.

"I have to go to sleep sometime," he said, listening to the strange sound of his own voice. "I can't stay awake forever!"

He yawned.

"Boys don't turn into girls," Marvin told General Jackson. "I'm just having strange thoughts because it's so late at night."

He looked at his clock. It was almost three thirty! He had school in five hours.

His eyes closed. He forced them back open.

"Casey Happleton is just a weird girl," he told the General.

General Jackson stuck out his tongue.

"My mother heard a scream in the night," Marvin explained to his lizard. "So *of course* she thought it was Linzy. Because Linzy is her little darling! That doesn't mean I sound like a girl!"

That made sense. Except his voice did sound different.

"I'm probably just getting a cold. From no sleep!"

He got on his knees. He bent his elbow around one of the legs of his desk chair. Then he tried to meet it from the other side with his mouth.

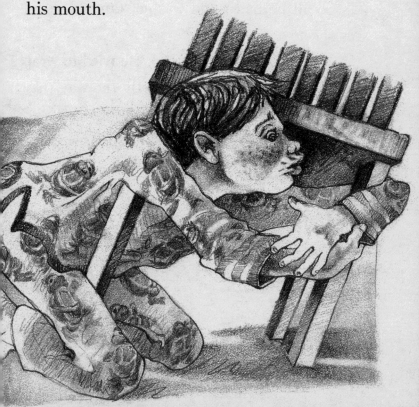

He tried another way.

He tried the other elbow.

"Casey Happleton is so weird!" he said.

He looked at his bed.

When he kissed his elbow the first time, he had been all tangled up in his sheets. Like a mummy.

So all he had to do was get tangled up in his sheets again!

He climbed back into bed. He tried to wrap the sheets around himself exactly the way they were before.

But the bed felt so good. The sheets so cozy.

He hugged his soft pillow. His eyes closed. He went to sleep.

Just like a caterpillar in a cocoon.

5

The Ugliest Face
in the World

Judy and Melanie were hanging upside down from the monkey bars.

"Hi, Marvin," said Judy. "Do you want to come to my slumber party?"

"Okay," said Marvin.

"Oh, goody," said Melanie. "We can stay up late and paint each other's toenails."

Marvin woke up.

"No!" he said, almost shouting.

He wanted to call Judy Jasper on the telephone and tell her he didn't want to go to her slumber party. And he didn't want to paint his toenails!

It was just a dream, he reminded himself.

A dream?

He wasn't supposed to go to sleep!

He jumped out of bed.

He checked himself over. He was still a boy.

He looked at his clock. 3:45. He had been asleep less than five minutes.

That wasn't enough time to turn into a girl.

He backed away from his bed and knocked over his desk chair. As he set it back up, he found himself staring at the ugliest face in the world!

He screamed.

He quickly covered his mouth.

It was just General Jackson. Safe in the glass cage.

That shouldn't have scared him. "I'm not afraid of a lizard," he said.

Girls are afraid of lizards.

He looked right into the eyes of General

Jackson. To prove he wasn't afraid.

"You don't scare me," he said.

General Jackson stuck out his tongue.

"How gross!" said Marvin.

He covered his mouth again.

Girls think lizards are gross.

"I don't think you're gross," he told the General. "I don't. I really don't. In fact, I think you're cute."

He covered his mouth.

Girls think lizards are cute.

He ran to the bathroom.

He looked at himself in the mirror.

He tried to look just at his face. Not the hair. Not the Ninja Turtle pajamas. Just his face.

It looked just the way it always did.

Except something about it was different. He rubbed his eyes. It was sort of . . . *pretty.*

He studied his face. He had a girl's nose!

As he looked at it from every angle, he became more and more sure of it.

"Oh my gosh," he said. He bit his finger.

"Hi, Marvin," Linzy said sleepily as she entered the bathroom.

Marvin could see her in the mirror. "Linzy, can I ask you something?" he said.

"Okay," said Linzy. She yawned.

"Okay, look at me," said Marvin. "This is real important."

He knelt down and put his hand on her shoulder. One thing good about little kids— they always told the truth.

"Look at my face," said Marvin. "Do I look like a girl?"

Linzy looked hard into his face. She touched his cheek. Then his ear. "Yes," she said.

"*What?*" exclaimed Marvin. "You're crazy, Linzy! That's stupid! You're just a stupid little kid!"

A frown slowly formed on Linzy's face.

"I'm sorry," said Marvin. "I'm sorry, Linzy."

But it was too late. She was crying.

"I'm sorry," Marvin said again. He sighed. "Okay. Why do you think I look like a girl?"

"You look like a boy," Linzy sobbed.

"Then why'd you say I looked like a girl?"

"I don't know," she said, still crying.

"You must have had a reason," said Marvin. "Just tell me. I won't get mad."

"I have to go potty," said Linzy.

Marvin waited while his sister used the bathroom. At least in that way, he knew he was still a boy.

"I'm sorry I yelled at you," he said when Linzy was through. "It's just—" He stopped. "If I tell you something, do you promise not to tell?"

Linzy promised.

"I think I'm turning into a girl," said Marvin.

Linzy's mouth dropped open. "I always wanted a sister!" she exclaimed, instantly happy. "That's what I wished for on my birthday cake. I blew out all the candles."

Marvin laughed.

"You'll be such a good sister, Marvin!" said Linzy. "We can play dress-up! And comb each other's hair. And you can teach me how to put on lipstick."

Marvin smiled at his sister. "We can have a tea party," he said.

"Yes!" said Linzy. "And no boys allowed!"

Marvin laughed.

Linzy laughed too.

In the middle of the night, Marvin and Linzy sat on the bathroom floor giggling at each other.

6
Off to School

"What happened to you?" Jacob asked when Marvin dragged himself downstairs in the morning.

"I didn't sleep too good," said Marvin.

He had stayed awake all night trying to kiss his elbow.

"More bad dreams?" asked his mother.

"I guess," Marvin muttered. He poured himself a bowl of cereal.

"Your voice sounds funny," said his mother. "Do you feel all right?"

"I think I'm getting a cold," he said. He hoped that's all it was.

Linzy smiled at him.

He stared down at his bowl of cereal. He had to hold his head up to keep from falling into it.

Ten minutes later Marvin was still staring at his bowl of soggy cereal.

"Pony or piggies?" asked his mother.

She was combing Linzy's hair.

"Piggies," said Linzy.

Marvin watched his mother give Linzy pigtails.

Girls are lucky, he thought. They could wear their hair in lots of fun ways. Pigtails. Ponytails. Bangs.

He liked bangs.

No, I don't! he told himself. *I don't like bangs. I don't want bangs. I don't want to wear my hair like a girl.* He didn't know why he had thought such a thought.

It was just that girls had longer hair, he decided. That was a fact. So they could wear their hair in lots of different ways. That was all there was to it. It didn't mean he wanted bangs.

Like the way girls dress. Boys just wore

pants. But girls were lucky. They could wear anything! Pants or skirts or dresses. And they could wear sparkles on their clothes. Boys didn't get to wear sparkles.

No! I don't want to wear sparkles! I don't want to wear a skirt or a dress! I like wearing pants.

"Mar-vin!" called Jacob. "Stuart and Nick are here."

"Oh my gosh," said Marvin. He bit his finger.

He walked to school with Nick and Stuart. He tried to act normal.

Nick had a loose tooth.

"Watch this," said Nick.

Nick opened his mouth wide. He pushed the tooth forward with his tongue, so that it almost lay down flat.

"Oh, gross!" said Marvin.

Nick and Stuart looked at him.

"I mean . . . cool!" said Marvin.

They got to school before class started.

"Look, there's Patsy Gatsby," said Nick.

Stuart laughed.

Patsy Gatsby was sitting alone playing jacks.

She was the weirdest girl in Marvin's class. Even weirder than Casey. Sometimes all you had to do was say her name, Patsy Gatsby, and everyone would laugh.

But Casey was funny-weird, Marvin thought. Patsy Gatsby was sad-weird.

She was always so quiet. Like she was afraid of people.

She didn't have any friends. No one ever talked to her.

Except Clarence. Clarence called her names. Worm-Face. Stupid-Head. Ugly. Double-Ugly. Stink-Girl.

Marvin watched her bounce the red ball, then pick up the little jacks.

He had never played jacks. It looked like a fun game.

"Where's your football?" asked Stuart.

"Huh?" said Marvin.

"Duh," said Nick.

Marvin suddenly remembered. He was supposed to bring his football.

"Now what are we going to do?" asked Stuart. "Play jacks with Patsy Gatsby?"

Nick laughed.

Marvin looked at Patsy.

Maybe she isn't the weirdest girl in class, he thought. *Maybe I am.*

He tried to think of another game to play. He didn't want to let his friends down.

Then he got a great idea. He didn't know why he had never thought of it before.

"Do you want to play hopscotch?" he asked.

7

It's Fun to Be a Girl

Marvin sat at his desk in Mrs. North's room.

He didn't see what was so bad about hop-scotch. He didn't know why Nick and Stuart had laughed at him.

It takes a lot of skill to play hopscotch, he thought. *Boys are just stupid!*

No, I don't mean that! he quickly told himself.

But girls were smarter than boys. That was a fact. Everybody knew that.

Or did they?

He couldn't remember if he used to think girls were smarter. Before he kissed his elbow.

He concentrated on his work.

He had been learning cursive writing.

He had the worst handwriting in the class. It was usually so bad, even he couldn't read it.

That was because he always wrote so fast.

But now, instead of rushing, he wrote each letter slowly and carefully.

Mrs. North walked past his desk. "Very nice, Marvin," she said.

Marvin smiled. It wasn't so hard to write neatly, he realized. If you just took your time.

He wrote each letter just the way he had been taught.

Except he didn't dot his *i*'s. Instead, over each letter *i* he drew a tiny heart.

He yawned.

He wished he could close his eyes for just a few seconds.

"Go to sleep, Marvin," said a voice inside his head.

It was a girl's voice.

"Close your eyes," the voice said softly. "You're halfway there."

He rubbed his eyes.

"What's wrong with turning into a girl?" asked the voice. "Girls are better than boys. Girls are smarter. Prettier. Braver. Girls can have ponytails. Pigtails. Bangs. Girls can wear sparkles on their clothes."

Marvin's eyes shut for a second, but he quickly opened them.

"Girls can do somersaults, Marvin. Your four-year-old sister can do a somersault, and you can't.

"Girls can hang from the monkey bars upside down by their knees."

Marvin had always wished he could do that.

"Girls can go into the girls' bathroom," said the voice. "Don't you want to go into the girls' bathroom? And hear all the secrets girls tell in there?"

Marvin wondered what girls talked about inside the girls' bathroom. They always came out giggling.

"They tell the most amazing secrets," said the voice. "No boy would ever understand."

His eyes closed.

He dreamed he was hanging from the monkey bars by his knees. A warm breeze blew in his face. Birds were singing.

He had long hair. It brushed against the ground.

He swung high off the monkey bars, did a somersault in midair, and landed on his feet.

His hair was shiny and silky. It hung over

his shoulders.

He shook his head. His hair swished from side to side.

He shook his head really fast. His hair whipped around.

He giggled.

It was fun to be a girl!

Out of the corner of his mouth he blew a few strands of hair off his face.

8
. . . A Little Different

He awoke to a loud cheer.

Casey Happleton was staring at him. "Oh my gosh," she said. She bit her finger.

"What?" asked Marvin.

"You fell asleep in class!" said Casey. Then she laughed.

Marvin shrugged.

He wondered how long he'd been asleep. And if he had changed at all.

He looked around. The other kids were all excited about something.

"Settle down," said Mrs. North, "or I'll have to change my mind."

"What happened?" asked Marvin.

"We get to go to Lake Park!" said Casey.

"Oh, goody!" said Marvin. He clapped his hands.

Casey looked at him funny. Her ponytail stuck out of the side of her head.

Marvin wondered what it would be like to have hair like that.

"What are you staring at?" asked Casey.

"Your ponytail," he said.

"What about it?" she demanded.

"It's cute," he told her. "But you always wear your hair the same way. If I had long hair, I think I'd wear pigtails sometimes. Or maybe a French braid."

Casey stared at him. "What's with you?" she asked.

"Nothing," said Marvin.

"And your voice sounds so funny," said Casey. "What'd you do? Kiss your elbow?"

He stared at her.

She stared back.

She knew.

He knew she knew.

She knew he knew she knew.

He knew she knew he knew she knew.

"No!" he said. "What do you think I am? Weird?"

Casey bit her finger.

The class had to pair up for the walk to Lake Park.

Lake Park was three blocks from school. It had a great playground.

Mrs. North sometimes took the class there on Friday if they'd been good all week. "Everyone find a partner," she said.

Marvin ducked under his desk. He pretended to tie his shoe. He was afraid to be partners with Nick or Stuart.

He needed to find a partner who didn't know him too well. Someone who wouldn't notice if he was . . . a little different.

He peeked out from under his desk.

Stuart and Nick were partners. Travis and Clarence. Kenny and Warren. Casey and Judy. Gina and Heather.

One person stood alone. Patsy Gatsby.

Kenny pointed at Patsy. "The cheese stands alone," he said.

Clarence held his nose. "And it's stinky cheese, too."

Patsy looked down at her shoes.

Marvin made his way across the room. "Would you like to be my partner, Patsy?" he asked.

For a moment Patsy didn't answer. Then, very quietly, she said, "Okay."

They got on the end of the line. Patsy kept her head down.

Stuart looked back at Marvin as if to ask, "What are you doing?"

Marvin shrugged. He saw Nick whisper something to Stuart. Then his two best friends laughed.

Warren sang:

> "Marvin and Patsy,
> Sitting in a tree,
> Kay-I-Ess-Ess-
> I-En-Gee "

Marvin looked at Patsy. She was blushing.

"Boys are so immature," said Marvin.

Patsy looked up and smiled at him.

She was wearing black suspenders over her pink T-shirt. Marvin thought it was a cute outfit.

Girls are lucky, he thought, as they walked to Lake Park. *They can wear anything. Even suspenders.*

But if I wore a dress to school, everyone would probably think I was weird or something.

Maybe not? He wasn't sure.

Maybe he should wear a dress to school

tomorrow, he thought. See what the other kids think.

Oh, I'm so silly, he suddenly realized. *There's no school tomorrow. Today's Friday.*

Patsy Gatsby was quietly humming to herself.

"Do you think it would be weird if I wore a dress to school?" Marvin asked her.

She looked up, then giggled.

Marvin giggled too.

He didn't know why he was giggling. It was fun just to laugh.

"In Scotland men wear skirts," said Patsy.

"Have you been to Scotland?" asked Marvin.

"No," said Patsy. "I read it in a book. The skirts are called kilts."

"You read a lot, don't you?" asked Marvin.

Patsy blushed. "I guess," she whispered. She

looked back down at her shoes.

"I see you playing jacks a lot, too," said Marvin.

Patsy shrugged.

"I've never played jacks," said Marvin.

"You like to play wall-ball," said Patsy.

Marvin was surprised she knew that. But then he knew she liked to play jacks. So why shouldn't she know he liked to play wall-ball?

"You should play wall-ball sometime," he suggested.

Patsy turned and looked at him. "No," she said, then looked back at her shoes.

"It's easy," said Marvin. "I can teach you."

Patsy didn't say anything.

"And you can teach me how to play jacks," said Marvin.

Patsy laughed. "You're funny, Marvin!" she said.

Marvin froze. He was afraid Patsy might have noticed something different about him. "What do you mean?" he asked.

"You're nice," said Patsy.

9

He Wouldn't Hit a Girl

Nick and Stuart were waiting for Marvin.

"How'd you get stuck walking with Patsy Gatsby?" asked Nick.

Marvin shrugged. He looked at Patsy. She was already walking away, head down.

"Was she weird?" asked Stuart.

"No," said Marvin. "We just talked."

"Ugh!" exclaimed Nick. "You talked to her!"

"C'mon," said Stuart. "Let's go climb the spiderweb."

The giant spiderweb was Marvin's favorite thing at Lake Park. It was made out of rope.

It was fun to climb, but scary. Especially way up at the top.

Marvin started toward it, then stopped and glanced back at Patsy.

She was sitting on the sidewalk. Playing jacks.

She didn't notice Clarence, Travis, and Kenny standing behind her.

She bounced the red ball.

Clarence kicked it. "Oops. Sorry, Worm-Face," he said.

Kenny and Travis laughed.

"C'mon, Marvin," said Nick, heading toward the spiderweb.

Marvin started after his friends, then stopped again.

He watched as Patsy tried to walk away from Clarence.

"What's the matter, Stink-Head?" asked

Clarence. He grabbed one of her suspenders.

"Let go," said Patsy.

Clarence pulled the suspender way back, then snapped it against her.

Travis and Kenny laughed.

Clarence grabbed her other suspender and snapped it, too.

"Quit it," said Patsy.

"Quit it," teased Clarence.

"Leave her alone!" said Marvin.

Clarence turned. "What's your problem, Redpost?"

Marvin marched right up to Clarence. "You think you're so tough, Clarence!" he said, hands on hips. "Well, you're not. You're just stupid and gross."

"I can beat you up," said Clarence.

"Oh, gee, I'm scared," said Marvin. He turned to Patsy. "Clarence thinks he's really great, just because he's the biggest kid in the

class. Well, the only reason he's so big is because he's been left back a hundred times."

Patsy laughed.

"I'm warning you," said Clarence.

A crowd gathered around them.

"Oh, grow up!" said Marvin.

Clarence glared at Marvin.

Marvin looked right back at him. Their faces were inches apart.

"I don't believe it," said Marvin. "You get uglier every day."

A group of girls laughed.

Clarence forced a laugh. He turned away. "You're not worth it," he said.

"All right, Marvin!" said Nick, slapping him on the back.

"Wow," said Stuart. "You stood up to Clarence."

Casey Happleton stared at him, finger in mouth.

"Weren't you scared?" asked Nick.

"No," said Marvin. "Clarence wouldn't hit—" Marvin stopped.

He was confused.

He was going to say, *Clarence wouldn't hit a girl.*

10

High Atop the Spiderweb

"Leave me alone," said Marvin. He walked away.

His friends followed.

"I said leave me alone!"

Everyone backed off.

Marvin climbed up the giant spiderweb.

The rope wiggled under his feet. The higher he got, the more the web seemed to wiggle and shake.

He reached the very top and looked down at the boys and girls in his class.

He was confused.

He had boy thoughts. He had girl thoughts. But he didn't know which were which.

Or did it matter? Was there really a difference in the way boys and girls thought?

He didn't know. He didn't know anything.

He was just very tired.

He watched Stuart and Nick chase Judy and Casey.

Judy sang out:

"Nick is rude.
Nick is crude.
Nick eats dog food!"

Then she ran.

Nick ran after her.

Then Marvin heard Casey sing:

"Stuart is rude.

Stuart is crude.

Stuart eats dog food!"

"I'm going to get you!" yelled Stuart.

Stuart chased Casey across the swinging bridge.

Nick chased Judy across the bridge from the other side.

The girls were trapped in the middle.

The boys moved in for the kill.

The girls screamed.

The boys stopped.

"Mrs. North!" yelled Judy. "Nick and Stuart keep bothering us."

Mrs. North made Nick and Stuart sit on the bench.

Marvin remembered he used to like to chase the girls too. He always thought the boys were in charge.

Now he knew. The girls *liked* to be chased.

It was a game. And the girls made all the rules. The boys could never win.

Boys are so stupid, he thought. He couldn't believe he used to be that stupid, too. It was embarrassing.

Suddenly his foot slipped off the rope. He almost fell, but grabbed a section of the rope just in time.

He pulled himself back up.

He looked around the play area. Clarence, Travis, and Kenny were hanging out. Patsy Gatsby was playing jacks. Casey and Judy were on the swings. Nick and Stuart were on the bench.

Suddenly Marvin understood.

"Oh my gosh!" he said. He bit his finger.

It all became clear to him.

He understood everything.

He knew what it felt like to be a boy.

He knew what it felt like to be a girl.

And now he knew the real difference between girls and boys. The *secret* difference!

He knew the one secret thing boys didn't understand about girls.

And he knew the one secret thing girls didn't understand about boys.

It was really very simple. The secret difference between girls and boys was—

Suddenly his foot slipped. He fell off the spiderweb.

11

Caught in the Web

But he never hit the ground.

Marvin found himself hanging upside down by his knees.

Just like Judy Jasper.

He let himself hang there a moment. It felt good.

Besides, he wasn't sure how to get free without falling the rest of the way.

"Hey, Marvin!" called Nick. "How'd you do that?"

"Marvin, are you all right?" called Mrs. North.

"I think so," he said.

He tried to get back up. He swung by his knees, reached out, and grabbed the web with one hand.

He wove his arm in and out of the web to get a good grip. Then he slowly freed one leg.

"Careful," said Mrs. North.

He pulled on the web with his free hand.

The next thing he knew, his elbow jerked almost to his mouth.

He pulled the web again.

Again his elbow jerked toward his mouth.

He pulled, then kept on pulling.

His elbow moved closer. It felt like his arm was breaking.

He stretched out his lips.

"What are you doing, Marvin?" Stuart called up to him.

It felt like his shoulder was about to pop out.

He gave it one hard yank!

The next thing he knew, he was falling headfirst toward the ground.

"Marvin!" screamed Patsy.

But as his head hit the sand, he kissed himself on the elbow.

"Marvin, are you okay?" asked Mrs. North.

"Are you all right, Marvin?" asked Patsy.

"Should we call an ambulance?" asked Stuart.

"Hey! Are you dead?" asked Clarence.

Marvin opened his eyes.

"I saw," said Casey.

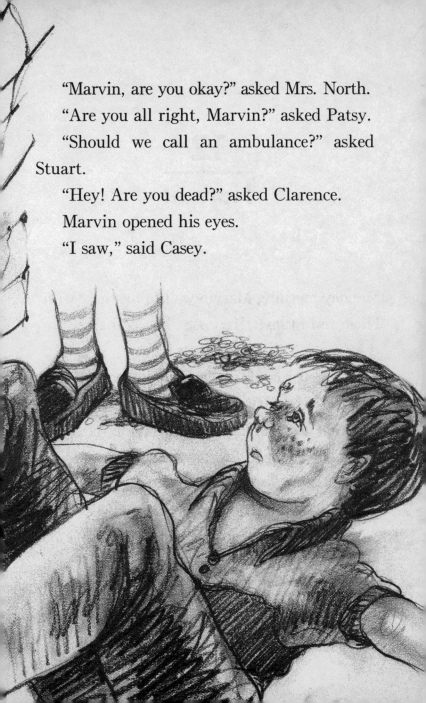

12
Normal

Monday morning Marvin walked to school with Nick and Stuart. He tossed his football up in the air.

He never could remember the *secret* difference between girls and boys.

That was silly anyway, he realized. *I just had weird thoughts because I was so tired.*

Boys don't turn into girls!

All he had needed was a good night's sleep. And then he was back to normal.

Except he really did have a cold. Which was why his voice sounded so strange.

Girls are just stupid and weird. That's the secret difference between boys and girls!

He entered his classroom. Clarence was sharpening his pencil.

Marvin suddenly remembered all the things he had said to Clarence at Lake Park.

I must have been out of my mind! I could have been killed!

He decided to apologize, just to be safe.

Clarence backed up when he saw Marvin. "What do you want?" he asked. He sounded nervous.

"Just, uh, sorry about Friday. I didn't get much sleep and I didn't know what I was saying." Marvin held out his hand. "Okay?"

Clarence smiled. He no longer seemed nervous. "Yeah, well, you're lucky I didn't knock your teeth out," he said. He shook Marvin's hand.

As Marvin walked to his desk, Clarence shoved him in the back.

"I saw you!" said Casey. "When you fell from the spiderweb. You kissed your elbow!"

"And I'm still a boy," said Marvin. "So that just proves you're weird!"

Casey sang very softly so only Marvin could hear:

"Marvin's rude.
Marvin's crude.
Marvin eats donkey food!"

"I'll get you at recess, Casey!" he said.

"Marvin?" said Mrs. North. "What was that?"

"Marvin won't quit bothering me," Casey complained. "He said he was going to get me at recess."

"Marvin, quit bothering Casey," said Mrs.

North. "I know she's pretty, but you need to keep your eyes on your book. Not on Casey."

Everyone laughed. Marvin turned red.

At recess he headed to the wall-ball court with Nick and Stuart.

"Look, there's Patsy Gatsby," said Nick.

Marvin and Stuart laughed.

Patsy Gatsby was playing jacks by herself.

Of all the weird things he did on Friday, Marvin thought, talking to her was the weirdest.

He shook his head. He remembered his conversation with her. She said he was *nice*.

Patsy looked up from her jacks. "Hi, Marvin," she said.

He walked right past her.

"Hi, Mar-vin," Stuart said with a funny voice as he gently shoved Marvin.

Nick laughed.

Marvin pushed Stuart back.

They got in line for wall-ball.

Marvin looked at Patsy. She didn't have any friends. Everyone just made fun of her.

"Hold my place," he said.

He went back to her.

He still thought jacks looked like a fun game. But he was embarrassed to play it.

"Hey, Patsy. Do you want to play wall-ball?"

Patsy quickly stuffed her jacks into her pocket. She came to the wall-ball court, all smiles.

"I promised I'd teach her how to play," Marvin explained to his friends.

"Hi," said Patsy.

"Uh, hi," said Stuart.

Nick grunted.